THE NIGHT BEFORE CHRISTMAS

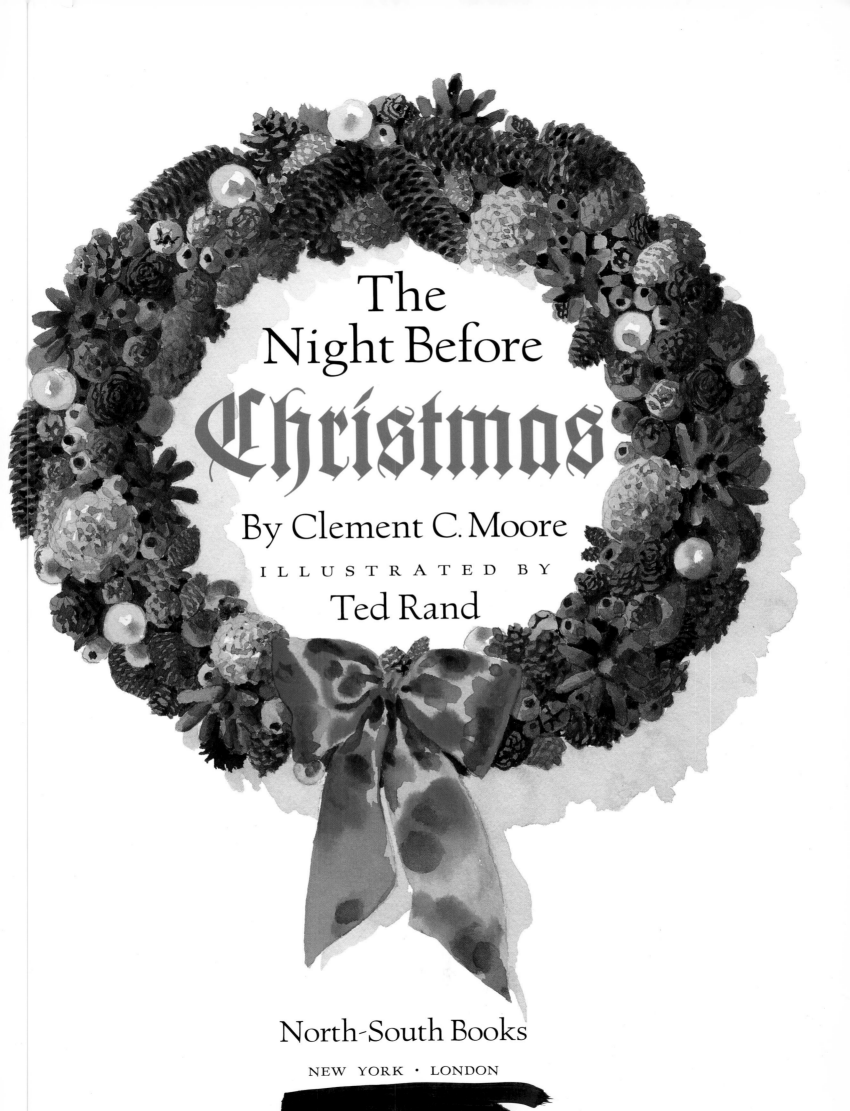

The Night Before Christmas

By Clement C. Moore

ILLUSTRATED BY

Ted Rand

North-South Books

NEW YORK · LONDON

'Twas the night before Christmas, when all through the house
Not a creature was stirring, not even a mouse.
The stockings were hung by the chimney with care,
In hopes that St. Nicholas soon would be there.

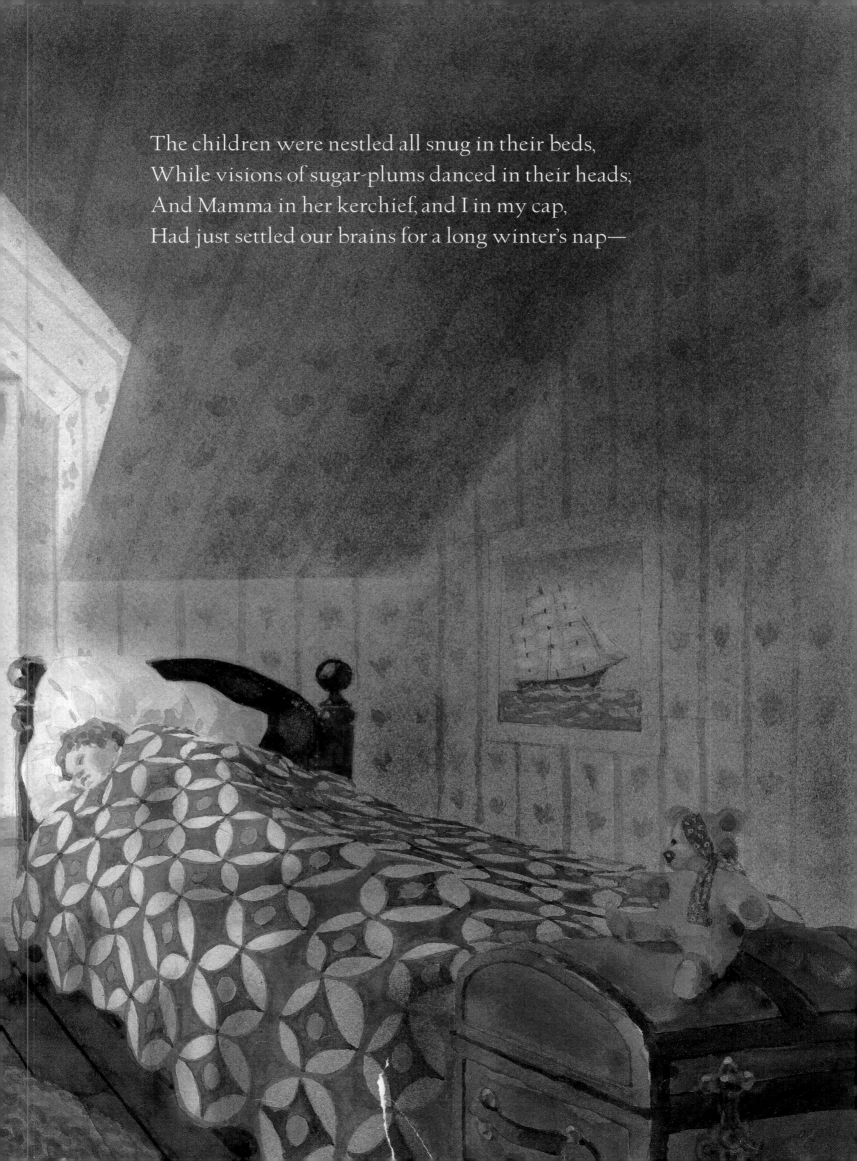

The children were nestled all snug in their beds,
While visions of sugar-plums danced in their heads;
And Mamma in her kerchief, and I in my cap,
Had just settled our brains for a long winter's nap—

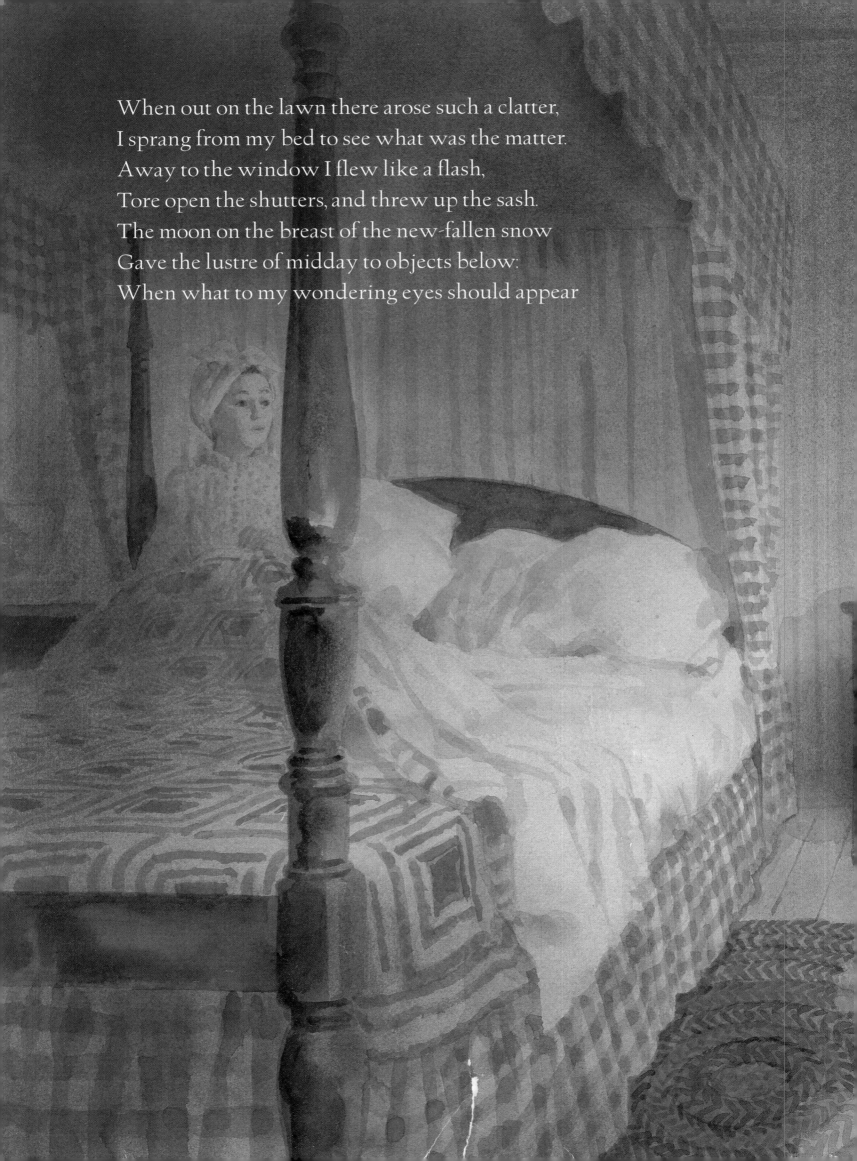

When out on the lawn there arose such a clatter,
I sprang from my bed to see what was the matter.
Away to the window I flew like a flash,
Tore open the shutters, and threw up the sash.
The moon on the breast of the new-fallen snow
Gave the lustre of midday to objects below:
When what to my wondering eyes should appear

But a miniature sleigh and eight tiny reindeer,
With a little old driver, so lively and quick,
I knew in a moment it must be St. Nick!
More rapid than eagles his coursers they came,
And he whistled and shouted and called them by name:

"Now, Dasher! now, Dancer! now, Prancer and Vixen!
On, Comet! on, Cupid! on, Donder and Blitzen!
To the top of the porch! to the top of the wall!
Now dash away! dash away! dash away all!"

As dry leaves that before the wild hurricane fly,
When they meet with an obstacle, mount to the sky,
So up to the housetop the coursers they flew,
With a sleigh full of toys, and St. Nicholas, too.
And then, in a twinkling, I heard on the roof
The prancing and pawing of each little hoof.
As I drew in my head and was turning around,

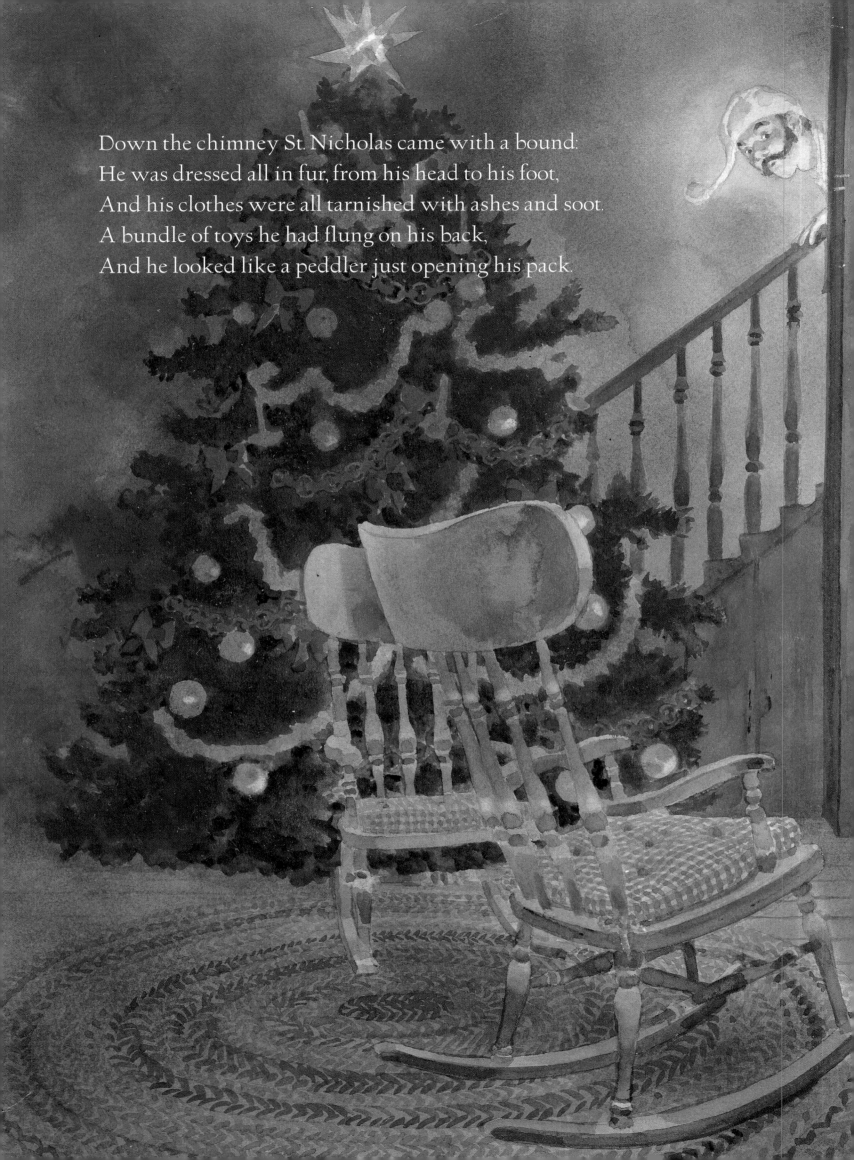

Down the chimney St. Nicholas came with a bound:
He was dressed all in fur, from his head to his foot,
And his clothes were all tarnished with ashes and soot.
A bundle of toys he had flung on his back,
And he looked like a peddler just opening his pack.

His eyes, how they twinkled! his dimples, how merry!
His cheeks were like roses, his nose like a cherry;
His droll little mouth was drawn up like a bow,
And the beard on his chin was as white as the snow.
The stump of a pipe he held tight in his teeth,
And the smoke, it encircled his head like a wreath.
He had a broad face and a little round belly
That shook, when he laughed, like a bowlful of jelly.
He was chubby and plump—a right jolly old elf:
And I laughed when I saw him, in spite of myself;
A wink of his eye, and a twist of his head,
Soon gave me to know I had nothing to dread.

He spoke not a word, but went straight to his work,
And filled all the stockings; then turned with a jerk,
And laying his finger aside of his nose,
And giving a nod, up the chimney he rose.

He sprang to his sleigh, to his team gave a whistle,
And away they all flew like the down of a thistle.
But I heard him exclaim, ere he drove out of sight,

"Happy Christmas to all,
and to all a good night!"

To Sierra and Luke

Published in the United States by North-South Books Inc, New York.
Published simultaneously in Great Britain, Canada, Australia, and
New Zealand in 1995 by North-South Books, an imprint of
Nord-Süd Verlag AG, Gossau Zürich, Switzerland.

Library of Congress Cataloging-in-Publication Data
Moore, Clement Clarke, 1779-1863.
The Night Before Christmas / by Clement C. Moore ; illustrated by Ted Rand.
Summary: Presents the well-known poem about an important Christmas visitor.
1. Santa Claus—Juvenile poetry. 2. Christmas—Juvenile poetry. 3. Children's poetry, American.
[1. Santa Claus—Poetry. 2. Christmas—Poetry. 3. American poetry. 4. Narrative poetry.]
I. Rand, Ted, ill. II. Title.
PS2429.M5N5 1995
811'.2—dc20 95-1775

A CIP catalogue record for this book is available from The British Library.

ISBN 1-55858-465-X (trade binding)
1 3 5 7 9 TB 10 8 6 4 2
ISBN 1-55858-466-8 (library binding)
1 3 5 7 9 LB 10 8 6 4 2
Designed by Marc Cheshire
Printed in Belgium